ANYTHING CAN HAPPEN,
YOU JUST HAVE TO BELIEVE!

Minerva Mint

capstone
young readers

Minerva Mint is first published in the United States in 2015 by
Capstone Young Readers
A Capstone Imprint
1710 Roe Crest Drive
North Mankato, Minnesota 56003
www.capstoneyoungreaders.com

Editorial project by Atlantyca Dreamfarm S.r.l.

Text by Elisa Puricelli Guerra; Translated by Marco Zeni
Illustrations by Gabo León Bernstein
Original edition published by Edizioni Piemme S.p.A., Italy
Original title: La città delle lucertole

International Rights © Atlantyca S.p.A., via Leopardi 8 – 20123 Milano – Italia —
foreignrights@atlantyca.it — www.atlantyca.com

Library of Congress Cataloging-in-Publication Data is available
on the Library of Congress website.

ISBN: 978-1-62370-179-6 (hardcover)
ISBN: 978-1-4342-9671-9 (library binding)
ISBN: 978-1-4342-9674-0 (paperback)
ISBN: 978-1-4965-0191-2 (eBook)

Summary:
The Order of the Owls' latest mission leads them to discover an underground city.

Designer:
Rick Korab

Printed in China.
032015   008866RRDF15

THE CITY OF LIZARDS

by Elisa Puricelli Guerra
illustrated by Gabo León Bernstein

TABLE OF CONTENTS

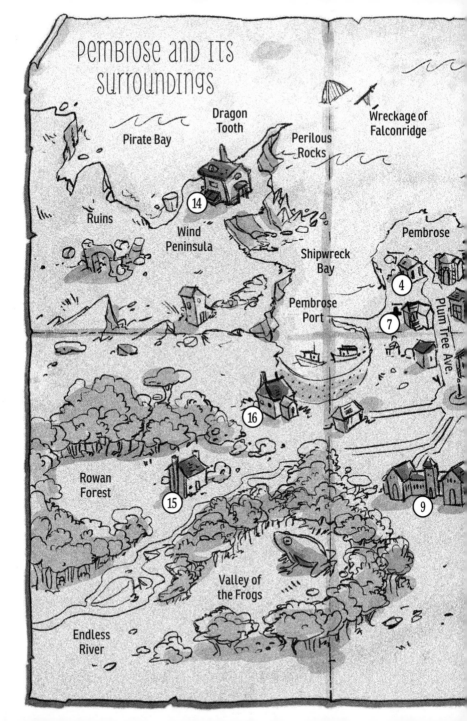

1. Lizard Manor
2. Crowley Hall
3. Smuggler's Den
4. Fishbone Inn
5. Post Office
6. Bon Ton Clothing Shop
7. Dr. Gerald's Clinic
8. Church
9. School
10. Gilbert O'Sullivan's House
11. Owl Tower
12. Agatha's Cottage
13. Tintagel Castle
14. The Lone Pirate Inn
15. Old House of Sighs
16. Fisherman Circle

WHAT'S HAPPENED SO FAR . . .

Minerva Mint is a nine-year-old girl living in Lizard Manor, atop Admiral Rock, in Cornwall, England. She lives with fourteen snowy owls, six foxes, and a badger named Hugo. She also shares her home with old Mrs. Flopps, the kind woman who found her in a bag at Victoria station in London when she was just a few months old.

Minerva is determined to find out what happened to her parents, but she only has a few clues to go on. The following items were left alongside her in the bag: a volume from the Universal Encyclopedia with a puzzle written on the first page ("Count the letters of Blue Tiger"); an envelope addressed to someone named Septimus Hodge, who actually does not exist; and the deed to the manor in Cornwall. For nine years, Minerva tried to unravel the mystery by herself, but now she finally has help: her friends Ravi and Thomasina.

The three friends have found a mysterious box containing a small flute. When the flute is played, dozens of snowy owls gather together. The words Ordo Noctuae are engraved on the box's lid. This translates to The Order of the Owl, which has become the name of their secret club. They even have a secret headquarters, Owl Tower, and an important mission: to solve the mystery of Minerva's origins.

The Order of the Owls have already discovered something very important: Minerva's ancestor was a member of the Ravagers of the Sea, a gang of ruthless pirates that used to wreak havoc on the coasts of Cornwall centuries ago. That means that she is entitled to part of their enormous treasure!

If only they could find it . . .

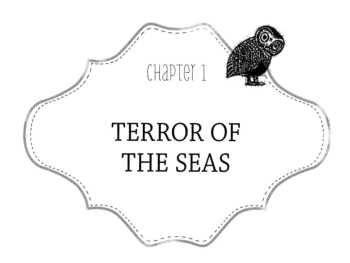

CHAPTER 1

TERROR OF
THE SEAS

I can't miss a chance like this! Minerva thought. It's much too good!

Silent as a fox, she laid her bicycle on the ground and crouched near a bush of blossoming honeysuckle. She took her slingshot out of her pocket and poised for action.

The O'Sullivans' small van was parked in their driveway. The family was about to leave for summer vacation. They were all in the van, including William the Conqueror, the vicious dog that was slobbering in the backseat. The only one still missing was . . .

"GILBERT!" Mrs. O'Sullivan yelled. "If you're not here in one minute, we're gonna leave without you!" she threatened, revving the engine and putting the car in gear.

Minerva pulled back the band of the slingshot and smirked. Gilbert O'Sullivan was the leader of a gang of bullies that terrorized all the children in the area. It was time for some payback.

"Jeez . . . I'm coming!" Gilbert snorted, trudging toward the van. He was covered in sweat and was carrying a bunch of tennis rackets. He bent down to put them in the trunk.

"Attaboy! That's it, don't move," Minerva whispered, closing one eye. "A perfect target . . ." She took aim and . . . "Bullseye!" she cheered.

An acorn hit Gilbert's bottom with a dry whacking sound.

"*Oww!*" the boy yelped.

"Gilbert, get in the car NOW!" his father ordered. "We're running late."

"But *Daaad* . . ." The boy was rubbing his aching

bottom when a second bullet hit him smack-dab on the nose.

"Ouch!" Gilbert yelled, scowling and searching for his tormentor.

Just then, the van started moving, and he could do nothing but jump in, without knowing who had dared to hit him. He did, however, have a suspect in mind. As a matter of fact . . .

"Enjoy your trip, Gilbert!" Minerva shouted, bouncing out from behind the bush the exact same moment the van pulled into the main road.

"Minerva Mint!" the boy roared. "I knew it was you!"

Minerva waved with the hand holding the sling-shot. "You know, I was feeling a bit rusty and thought I'd get some practice. Thanks for volunteering as a target!" she said, taking a bow. "Come back soon! I get bored when you're not around."

"I'll get you for this next time . . . I . . . I . . ." Gilbert bellowed. But the van disappeared round a curve, and his threats faded in the wind.

With a chuckle, Minerva put the slingshot away. She had made the handy thing herself, and it had never missed a shot so far.

To limber up after her victory, she did a couple of cartwheels and some leaps.

"Now that's the perfect way to celebrate the beginning of the summer!" she exclaimed, pausing to take a breath. Then she did one last cartwheel, just to round it all off.

Truth be told, there was nothing more exciting than the beginning of the summer break. It made Minerva feel like singing, dancing, doing a million cartwheels . . . even if she did not actually go to school. However, her friends Ravi and Thomasina did, and from that day on, she was going to have them all to herself. And that was a good reason to celebrate!

Minerva was supposed to meet them downtown in front of the post office on Plum Tree Avenue. Their plan was to buy a bunch of delicious things to eat and spend the whole afternoon at their secret hideout in the moorland.

What a perfect plan! Minerva thought, jumping on her bicycle and zipping along the path that led to Pembrose. Her red curls danced in the wind, and she yelled, "Out of my way!" just in case some unfortunate fellow happened to be standing in her path.

* * *

Pembrose was a tiny village, neatly nestled into a crystal clear bay dotted with toy-sized fishing boats. Smoky gray seals lazed in the sun, while squeaking puffins and seagulls circled the harbor. Charming cottages, so close together that they looked like sardines in a box, lined the steep cobbled streets that rose from the ocean.

Tourists swarmed to the sleepy village in July. That year, Merlin's book of prophecies had been discovered nearby. It was now kept at the little museum by the harbor, and the number of visitors had skyrocketed as a result. Spotting tourists was an easy task: all you had to do was look for the cameras and the noses, which were reddened and a little burned by the sun that had been shining brightly in the clear blue sky for days.

Because of the large amount of tourists, the mayor had closed the city center off to cars. Built hundreds of years before, its narrow streets were meant for pack mule transport. If they were carrying heavy bags, the tourists could always ask for a ride from Lola, a laid-back pinto horse that pulled a small wagon driven by Timothy, the shy owner of the Fishbone Inn, the only hotel and restaurant in the village.

"Out of my way!" Minerva yelled, shooting like a bullet down Plum Tree Avenue. She was not very good at slowing down.

Some of the more athletic tourists managed to get out of her way, but in order to avoid a group of people gathered in front of the post office, she had to swerve wildly. Luckily for her, she ended up in a heap of hay bales outside the Fishbone Inn.

I really need to work on my technique, Minerva thought, lying spread eagle on the hay. "Um, hi Lola," she said to the horse that was carefully looking at her with big hazelnut eyes. "I'm really sorry I messed up your lunch," Minerva apologized.

Ravi's and Thomasina's faces popped up next to Lola's muzzle. "Minerva, are you all right?" they asked with worry. "Did you break anything?"

Minerva smiled. "Never been better!" she answered. And to prove that she was telling the truth, she immediately jumped to her feet.

To her great surprise, she realized that the whole village had witnessed her "accident." There was Timothy and Lola the horse, the two Bartholomew sisters, the local police officer Oliver, Ravi's mother (who ran the post office), Doctor Gerald, and the old vicar Father Trout, plus a bunch of old fishermen and spinsters of varying ages, who made up the vast majority of Pembrose's population.

Oh boy, I'm in trouble now! Minerva thought, glancing worringly at Oliver. The officer had already complained about her reckless riding. He had even called her "public enemy" once.

However, no one paid any attention to her. It seemed like they were in the middle of an important discussion.

"What are all these people doing here?" Minerva whispered to her friends.

Thomasina whispered back, "There's a mystery!"

Minerva's freckled face brightened. "Really?"

"Well, we still don't know if it's a *real* mystery," Ravi added.

Thomasina looked perfect in her school uniform, which looked awful on any other schoolgirl. Her soft blond curls were held together by a hairband, and her patent leather shoes were spotless. But there was very little grace in the way she elbowed Ravi. "Aw, shush! Don't spoil it for everyone as usual!" she snapped.

He was just about to snap back when loud voices coming from the little crowd caught his attention.

"It's the third night in a row that she ripped up my nets!" an old sailor yelled.

"Ours too!" chimed a group of fishermen.

"I saw something in the water," said Joe, the museum guard. "A dark shape. It was huge . . ."

"I saw it too!" Oliver cried. "While I was on the beat out by the harbor. There was something huge, something monstrous . . ."

"That's the Terror of the Seas!" old Ms. Mackerel cried. "What else could be wandering about out there at night in the open water?"

Everyone's face turned pale.

"But . . . that's a sign of great misfortune," one of the sailors mumbled, voicing everybody else's fears. The people from Pembrose were very superstitious.

"Aye," Mr. Herring, the retired commodore, said in a grim tone. "Last time it showed up in Cornwall, all the fish died, and the nets went empty for years."

"Oh, come on! There's surely another reasonable explanation." Doctor Gerald's voice cut clear though the chatter. The town doctor was a man of great wisdom, and in addition to relying on him for both real and imaginary ailments, the people from Pembrose held his opinion in high regard.

Minerva, Ravi, and Thomasina eagerly listened to every single word. But they were suddenly distracted by something dark and furry jumping on them and pushing them down.

"Pendragon!" Ravi cried.

The dog started licking his face and then did the same to the two girls.

"Excuse him, he's very happy to see you," a gentle voice said.

The three kids' eyes rose and set on a porcelain white face and two eyes that were as blue as the water of a moor pond.

"Agatha!" they shouted in unison.

"Be a nice boy, Pendragon. Let them breathe at least," the young woman told the dog. With a gentle movement, she took him and picked him up. "Hello, children. It's been a long time, hasn't it?" She smiled, and her face lit up with beauty. "I came down to buy some thread for my needlework, but I wasn't expecting to find the whole town here." She sighed, looking around.

Some of the people saw her and took a couple of steps back. Others glanced nervously at her.

Agatha Willow, the rumored witch of Bodmin Heath Moor, was not very popular in Pembrose. So she chose to live all alone in a cottage out by Alder Swamp, where she mixed medicines from the wild plants that grew all around.

"Agatha, there's a mystery!" Minerva said, too excited to give their friend a proper greeting.

"Something called the Terror of the Seas has been ripping the sailors' nets apart," Thomasina added.

"Do you know anything about it?" Ravi asked.

Agatha had already helped them solve another mystery. They had discovered Merlin's Cave, thanks to her.

"Does the Terror of the Seas really exist?" Minerva added.

Agatha sighed. "Children, do you remember when I told you old legends are best left alone?"

"Yes, but when we didn't listen, we found Merlin's Book of Prophecies!" Minerva promptly replied.

Agatha burst into laughter. The Order of the Owls wouldn't give up and would learn everything about the Terror of the Seas, with or without her.

"All right," she gave in. "I'll tell you what I know, but I need a favor in return. Would you mind looking after Pendragon for a couple of days?" she asked, stroking the dog's furry head. "Tristam and I are going to look at a castle in Scotland, and I can't take Pendragon with me."

Tristam was the young archaeologist who, just a month earlier, had caused quite a fuss in the village when he claimed that Merlin's Cave did not exist, only to change his mind shortly after. His change of heart was in no small part due to the beauty of the witch from the moor.

"It's a deal!" Ravi said, immediately pulling the dog into his lap. Pendragon gleefully lapped the boy's face.

"Thank you." Agatha smiled. "I'm warning you, though . . ." Her blue eyes turned somber. "If it really is the Terror of the Seas . . . *no one* will stand a chance."

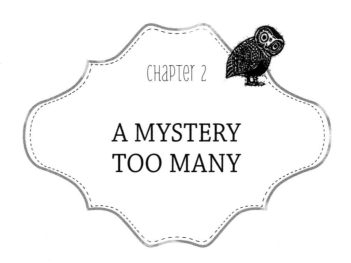

CHAPTER 2

A MYSTERY
TOO MANY

Three bicycles zipped through Bodmin Heath Moor, the wildest place in Cornwall. Crouched inside Ravi's bicycle basket, Pendragon admired the scenery, his big ears flapping in the wind.

"You've never been on a bike, have you?" Ravi whispered, leaning over the handlebar to pet him. "We're going to Owl Tower now. You're going to like it, you'll see. We're going to make a nice dog house for you."

"Hey, Ravi!" Thomasina yelled. "When did you turn into a snail?"

Ravi looked up and realized his friends were way ahead of him. They were racing, and it looked like Thomasina was leading, though by just a little.

The boy leaned down to talk to the dog. "Hold on Pendragon!" he said, pedaling like crazy. "We're going to fly now!" He caught up with the others in no time and with a last effort, he passed them. "See?" he cried to Pendragon. "*I'm* the fastest!"

His edge on them was not going to last long, though. They were hot on his heels and kept closing in. They had no intention of letting him win the race.

Summer had broken out all around them. Thousands of pink flowers had blossomed in the recent warm weather, dotting the emerald-green meadows. The deeper the children ventured into the moor, though, the more barren the landscape grew. There wasn't a soul down there, except for wild ponies that ran free on the hills and a couple of lonely sheep. The only sound was the hissing wind that, over the centuries, had formed the tors — strange and spookily shaped granite boulders. On that day, the wind tousled the purple sea of heather and rippled the moor pond's surface, upon which ducks bobbed.

Once their hideout was in sight, the kids slowed their pace. Owl Tower had a very peculiar look. Ball-shaped at the bottom, it grew narrow toward the top, like a vase. It was carefully positioned so you could see everything from its windows: to the west you could see the shiny ocean and Tintagel, the castle of legendary King Arthur. To the east were the gloomy hills of High Moore, and in the back stood Brown Willy, Cornwall's highest and most dangerous spot.

They hid their bicycles under a bunch of dried heather branches and entered the tower.

As they walked up the stairs, Thomasina blurted out, "Boy, another mystery — just when the Order of the Owls have their hands full with the mystery of the missing treasure!" For her, there were never enough mysteries and adventures.

"That's right. We're going to have to work extra hard," Minerva happily agreed.

Ravi snorted and buried his face in Pendragon's soft fur. For him, two mysteries were two mysteries too many.

Ravi could barely manage to carry Pendragon up the stairs. So he was happy to reach the top and finally lay the dog down onto one of the comfortable silk cushions that Thomasina had scooped up by the armful from her own house.

"I'll get you something yummy to nibble on now," he told the dog. Then he slapped himself on the forehead. "Oh no! We forgot to buy our snacks!"

Their headquarters was usually fully stocked with everything necessary: not only sleeping bags, flashlights, binoculars, a first aid kit, and three slingshots — which Minerva had made herself — but also a basketful of cookies and fruit juice. That day, however, when Ravi peeked into the basket, he found it empty.

"How about a scone?" Thomasina offered, as she reached into her inseparable bag and took out three sweet-smelling, warm blueberry scones, baked by Crowley Hall's experienced chef.

Ravi immediately gave a piece of his to Pendragon, who seemed to appreciate the gesture; in one single bite he also swallowed the part that Ravi had meant to keep for himself.

The boy turned to ask Thomasina if she had another scone. But his friend, after wiping her mouth with a delicate lace napkin, gracefully sat down on a cushion next to Minerva and said, "Let's get to work."

That's just perfect, Ravi thought. *Now I have to face* two *adventures on an empty stomach!* He hugged Pendragon, seeking some comfort. After all, the dog was named after an ancient Cornish king, famous for his courage.

Thomasina cleared her throat. "Okay, Agatha told us that the Terror of the Seas is a legendary sea monster," she began. "Some say it looks like a crab. Some say it looks like a jellyfish, and some say it looks like an octopus." Full of excitement, she stood up and widened her arms "They all agree on the fact that it is HUGE. So huge that you can mistake it for an island when it surfaces."

At that thought, they all fell silent.

How big is an island? Ravi wondered. Too big for his liking. He could already picture himself, dragged by the other two, aboard a tiny boat on their way to confront the monster.

"It lies asleep at the bottom of the ocean," Thomasina resumed. "But every hundred years it wakes up. That's when it emerges and —"

Minerva shot to her feet. "And when it emerges, it sprays water from its dreadful nostrils," she cried, splashing her glass of orange juice all around. "And it causes whirlpools so powerful that even the biggest ships are sucked down into the abyss!"

"And its tentacles are so long and strong," Thomasina added, "that it can wrap up ships and crush them!" She snapped a stick she had picked up.

Ravi covered his ears. He didn't want to hear anything more.

Thomasina crouched in front of a bookshelf where they kept books about adventures and other spectacular stories. She pulled out a large volume and started leafing through it. "I brought this from Crowley Hall library," she explained. "It's the *List of Mythical and Extraordinary Creatures.*"

She looked at the table of contents. "Let's see . . . Terror of the Seas. Here it is! There's a picture too!"

Minerva immediately joined her, and even Ravi could not resist. Three pairs of uneasy eyes were gazing at a clawed and long-tentacled sea monster shown crushing a ship. Tiny, terror-stricken sailors jumped overboard and dove into the billows, while the monster dragged the ship down into the abyss.

Ravi snapped the book shut. "Okay. It's a deal. We're going to leave the Terror of the Seas alone!"

"Huh?" asked Thomasina.

"What?" shouted Minerva.

Ravi crossed his arms. Agatha's words echoed in his mind: *If it really is the Terror of the Seas . . . no one will stand a chance.* Those two had no sense of danger whatsoever. Therefore, it was up to him to save them. The question was: how? "I'd like to remind you that I

can't swim," he said finally. "Besides, we have a very important mystery to solve. Or did you forget?"

Minerva shook her head and toyed with the golden key that she kept around her neck along with the tiny flute she always had with her.

They had found the key in Lizard Manor behind the portrait of Merrival M., Minerva's pirate ancestor. Minerva and the pirate looked like two peas in a pod. Almost three centuries before, that red-haired and green-eyed man had plundered and sunk traveling ships along the Cornish coast. He and his crew were known as the Ravagers of the Sea, and they were led by the evil Black Bart. The gang included a mysterious woman named Althea. One day, however, Black Bart had betrayed her and sent her to die in the Tower of London, thus calling upon himself a curse that was supposed to haunt him for centuries.

The key was believed to open the door to the City of the Ravagers, where a fabled treasure was hidden. To find it, though, the Order of the Owls would have to solve a rather complex puzzle first.

Ravi took out a crumpled piece of paper from his jeans pocket and read:

When the owl is cut in half,

And the lizard loses its tail,

You have found the City of the Ravagers.

Go there now or it'll disappear in one hour.

The piece of paper was scribbled all over with their futile attempts at solving the puzzle. They had been working on it for a whole week — in vain.

"We must figure out what it means," the boy said, and then he was distracted by Pendragon who was trying to eat the piece of paper.

Thomasina let herself fall back on a pillow. "Rats! This puzzle is driving me crazy!" she snorted.

Minerva sat next to her. "Well, the more difficult the mystery, the better. Don't you think?" she tried to console her.

"That's right," Ravi said. He was happy some-one was on his side. "Besides, if one of Minerva's ancestors was one of the Ravagers of the Sea, a share of the treasure belongs to her. So we *have* to find it!

We'll search every inch of Lizard Manor. If the key was hidden behind a painting in the portrait gallery, then maybe the door to the City of the Ravagers is in the house too," he suggested.

"You're right!" a perky Minerva said. "It could be one of the three I haven't found yet."

Lizard Manor was a huge house with fifty-five rooms, three of which no one could find the door to.

Thomasina propped herself on her elbows. "That is probably a good idea," she admitted, a bit more enthusiastically.

Minerva flashed an encouraging smile. Then she looked at Ravi: a feisty light was shining in her green eyes. "I'm warning you, though, if the Terror of the Seas threatens Pembrose," she said with conviction, "he's gonna have to deal with the Order of the Owls!"

The boy sighed. "Okay," he promised. He glanced at the ocean outside the window and made a silent plea to the waves. *Terror of the Seas, whoever you are, please stay away from Minerva, or we're all going to be in big trouble!*

CHapter 3

CORNWALL'S TERROR

WHOOOSH!

A cloud of soot puffed out of the fireplace in the Red Dame Room and covered the members of the Order of the Owls, plus Pendragon, who had joined them to help with the search.

"*Achoo!*" Minerva sneezed, shaking her curls that were now completely black.

They were all as black as coal now.

"*Achoo!*" Thomasina echoed.

"*Achoo!*" Ravi replied.

They looked at each other and couldn't help but

burst into laughter. Their teeth were still white at least.

Minerva wiped the golden key clean. "Well, I'd say there are no doors in this chimney," she said.

"We've been looking all day," Thomasina moaned, "and we haven't found it yet!"

"Of course we haven't. This house is so big!" Ravi reminded her. "We could try the basement." By no means was he going to let Thomasina give up and start thinking about the monstrous squid that haunted the waters around Pembrose.

At that exact moment, someone knocked on the door. *BOOM! BOOM! BOOM!* The ancient house shook with the sound of three strong knocks.

"Who could that be?" a surprised Minerva exclaimed. Nobody ever showed up at Lizard Manor.

Reaching the front door meant walking through many rooms, and since the electricity did not work properly, they had to do it in the dark. They each took a candle and went down the creaking stairs.

Keeping a big house clean was not an easy task.

And clean it definitely was not. Huge and intricate cobwebs made it difficult for them to move around. Ravi closed his eyes to block out the sight of the little eight-legged creatures that scurried around, as well as the portraits of Minerva's ancestors — portraits that made him feel more and more uncomfortable. He swallowed as he listened to the eerie sounds around him. Lizard Manor was cloaked in a weird mystery. It had not one, not two, but many secrets, and it guarded them very closely.

The hallway was tight; it was filled by a huge suit of armor that was missing an arm and a leg. While he was rushing to get to the door first, Pendragon bumped into the armor, causing the other arm to fall. It clanged and rolled outside as Minerva opened the door.

A tall, bulky woman picked up the metal arm. In spite of the hot weather, she was wearing a Scottish tweed dress and thick wool socks. She laid the arm next to a small statue of a lizard that sat on the edge of a water fountain just outside the front door.

"Good morning. My name is Amelia Broomstick," she said. She peered at them from behind the shiny lenses of her glasses. "*Hmph*, you're as dirty as dishwater," she said solemnly, showing her disgust.

"We had a little problem with the fireplace," Ravi explained.

"*Humph*. Is that so?" the woman said. She reached into her briefcase, took out a crocodile-skin notepad, and jotted down some notes with a fountain pen.

Her steel gray hair was pulled back so tightly on top that it looked like she was smiling. When she looked at the children, though, she was not smiling at all. "Who of you three is Minerva Mint?" she snapped.

Feeling left out, Pendragon let out a long howl.

"*Humph*," the woman snorted. "Dirty animal. No muzzle," she muttered, taking notes. "Are there more?"

Minerva thought for a moment. "Do fourteen snowy owls on the roof count?" she asked.

At that moment, a large fox darted through the door, followed by four smaller ones and another bigger one.

"*Humph.* Foxes?" Mrs. Broomstick snorted. "Were they given anti-rabies shots?" she inquired.

"Who are you?" Thomasina asked in that haughty tone that was typical of the members of her upper-class family. Her family was of noble birth.

The woman stood at attention like a soldier. "Amelia Broomstick. First-class social worker. London Office, Good Manners Alley, age 51. I am looking for Minerva Mint."

"That's me," Minerva responded. She tried, without success, to wipe the soot off her hand and politely held it out to the woman.

After looking at Minerva as if she were a rotting worm, the woman ignored her. "I am here on behalf of the London Central Office. Unfortunately, your file has never been processed, because it was stuck in a narrow gap between the wall and a file cabinet in Section 4B: Child Custody. Therefore, nobody bothered with it for nine years. However, I am now here to make up for that," she concluded. "May I please speak with Mrs. Flopps?"

Minerva hesitated for a moment. Mrs. Flopps had gone to the farmers' market in Truro to sell her homemade jams. She planned to be away for a couple of days. Something, however, told Minerva that she better not mention that to Mrs. Broomstick, first-class social worker.

"She can't see you now," she replied. "She's cleaning the chimney. It's going to take a while." She felt a familiar tickle at her feet (telling lies always made her feet feel funny), but she managed not to laugh.

"*Humph,* I see," Mrs. Broomstick said. "In that case, I shall begin my inspection without her." She held up her bag. "I have your file here. At the moment, it's the only copy. When I am finished with this inspection, I'll save all the data on my computer," she explained. "May I come in please?" Without waiting for an answer, she pushed the kids inside and closed the door behind her.

"*Humph,*" was her first reaction as she glanced around the entrance hall. Lizard Manor never made a good impression on its visitors. This time, however, it made a very *bad* impression.

"Why is it so dark in here?" she asked.

And that was just the first of an endless series of questions.

With a military-like attitude, Mrs. Broomstick explored room after room. The shiny crocodile-skin boots she wore creaked eerily with every step she took, echoing throughout the house.

Nothing escaped the eyes behind the lenses of her glasses. And whenever she saw something she did not like, she would snort, "*Humph*," which meant no good news at all. Her notepad was soon filled with notes as black as the night itself. Ravi managed

to catch a couple of words here and there: *hovel,*
extremely dangerous, and *spiders the size of an onion.*

When Mrs. Broomstick ran into Hugo the badger, one of the other tenants of the house, she let
out three gruff *humphs* in a row. A very bad sign.

And when she saw the yellow tent Minerva slept in, she let out an extremely loud *HUMPH!*

"*Humph,* that's enough for one day," she said finally, snapping her notepad shut.

"About time," Ravi whispered to his friends. When the lady had entered the house, their search had been put on hold.

"I'll have to come back tomorrow," the social worker added. "This house is enormous."

Three pairs of desparate eyes met each other. Mrs. Broomstick was a real pain in the neck!

"*Humph,* I do hope Mrs. Flopps will grace me with her presence . . ." The lady snorted, wiping a piece of cobweb off her sleeve. She turned on her heel, walked out, and headed for the village, marching to the military creaking of her boots.

"What are we going to do now?" Ravi asked. They looked at each other. They were all still as black as coal.

"When I go back home today, I'll have to climb up the wisteria tree to get inside," Thomasina said.

"If my parents see me like this, they're going to have a heart attack!"

"Yeah," Minerva sighed. "And this is how I looked when that social worker found me!"

Ravi looked at her. "You think she'll take you to London?" he asked, concerned.

Thomasina opened wide her big blue eyes. "Oh no! Is she going to say that this house is not suitable for a little girl and send you to stay with someone else?"

Minerva was silent for a moment. Then she shook her tangled curls, spreading soot all around. "She might want to do that . . ." she said with a smirk. "But I won't let her!"

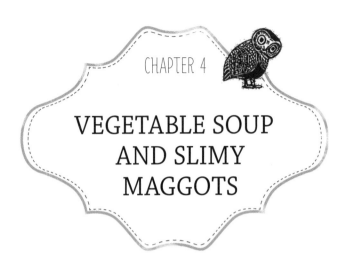

CHAPTER 4

VEGETABLE SOUP AND SLIMY MAGGOTS

Ravi was keeping watch behind a large flower bush next to Lizard Manor's rickety gate. It was so hot that July morning that he had dozed off, but an eerie creaking suddenly woke him up.

SQUEEEAK! SQUEEEAK!

"Shoot, here she comes!" Ravi exclaimed as he scanned the path that came up from Admiral Rock.

He took a hand mirror from his pocket and with shaking fingers pointed it toward the sun.

Ever since the friends had learned Morse Code,

the members of the Order of the Owls had been using it as their secret code to communicate from a distance. They used mirrors to send signals.

A reflection that lasted a very short time meant a dot, while a reflection that lasted three times as long was a dash. The alphabet was made up of various combinations of dots and dashes.

The message that Ravi was now desperately trying to send was "Danger."

How many dots are there in a D? he wondered. *Are there two dots or two dashes in an R?* He was trying so hard to remember that he forgot to point the mirror toward the third-floor window, where Minerva was keeping watch. He pointed it at the lawn instead.

SQUEEEAK! SQUEEEAK! The crocodile-skin boots were getting closer.

Ravi's head was so full of dots and dashes that he completely stopped watching where he was pointing the mirror.

Meanwhile, perched upon the roof, fourteen snowy owls observed the unusual scene.

Like a bunch of wise old men, they rolled their yellow eyes and shook their fluffy heads. Something bad was about to happen.

Sure enough, smoke had begun to rise from a narrow patch of dry grass that had been hit by the sunlight concentrated by the mirror.

Ravi, however, was looking at the window where Minerva was keeping watch. He did not realize what was happening. "Come on, Minerva," he begged. "Why can't you see my signal?"

A little flame flickered out of the smoking grass.

Augustus, the biggest among the owls, took off, flapping his majestic wings.

The tiny flames multiplied, and the lawn was soon ablaze with a crackling fire.

The owl zeroed in on Ravi's head. Frightened, the boy dropped the mirror.

"Augustus!" the boy moaned. "I can't play with you now!" That was when he finally saw the fire. He darted toward the lawn, screaming like a madman, "Fire! Fire! Help! Minerva, Thomasina! Fire! *Heeelp!*"

The two girls rushed to the scene of the disaster, followed by a woofing Pendragon.

"I set the lawn on fire!" Ravi screamed, horrified.

And that is how Mrs. Broomstick found them when she finally walked through the gate and stopped to observe the show, her hands on her large hips.

"*Humph,* this is going from bad to worse!" she grumbled. Calm and collected, she took off her heavy tweed coat and tossed it on the flames, smothering the fire. Then she examined the coat to assess the damage and let out a resigned *hmph*. The coat was as good as gone. "Where is Mrs. Flopps?" she asked Minerva.

The eyes that stared at Minerva from behind the spotless glasses were terrible, but Minerva was afraid of nothing.

"She is polishing the basement floor," she responded, wriggling her toes inside her boots to suppress her laughter. "She does it every month."

"*Humph*," Mrs. Broomstick said suspiciously. "In that case, I'll have to proceed without her." She marched into the house.

Thomasina scowled at Ravi. "Well done! Now we're in really big trouble!" she said.

They had agreed to take turns watching for the social worker so that they would be ready for her. But they had been anything but ready when she appeared.

Ravi blushed. In spite of her haughty and unbearable attitude, Ravi had a huge crush on Thomasina, and his heart ached whenever she yelled at him.

"The Morse Code is too difficult . . ." He was scrambling for some kind of excuse. "And dangerous," he added, looking at the strip of scorched lawn.

"Sure," the girl said sarcastically. "Especially if you can't point the mirror in the right direction . . ."

"CHILDREN!" Mrs. Broomstick called. "Where is the light switch in this house?"

* * *

The next two days were the same. The social worker came to the house both in the morning and in the afternoon. When she wasn't there, she could be found at the Fishbone Inn. Unfortunately, she seemed totally unaffected by Timothy's fish stew, which was known for causing instant diarrhea. That woman had a cast-iron stomach!

Every time she showed up, Minerva scrambled to find a new excuse to justify the absence of Mrs. Flopps.

"No, she can't see you, she's fixing the bed . . ."

"No, she's busy. She's redecorating the attic . . ."

"No, she's picking raspberries on the slopes of Traitor's Rock . . ."

The girl's toes tickled more than ever. Therefore, to avoid bursting into laughter, she forced herself to think of horrible, disgusting things.

Her friends tried to help her.

"Think about eating a whole bowl of stinky brussel sprout soup," Ravi whispered to her.

"Or about a thousand cockroaches crawling in your hair," Thomasina whispered.

"Or about falling into a pool of rotten eggs full of slimy crawling maggots," Ravi whispered at the umpteenth question about Mrs. Flopps. And he smiled, pleased with himself. He thought that was the yuckiest idea of them all.

"Rats! How are we supposed to find the door with Mrs. Broomstick always snooping around!" Thomasina fumed.

Since it was lunchtime, they decided to make the best of it and bought themselves a traditional Cornish specialty — pastry pies filled with meat and onions.

They ate at the Pembrose wharf, dipping their feet in the water to fend off the heat. Nestled like a precious stone between the sheer cliffs, the turquoise ocean looked as smooth as silk, the water surface rippled only by the occasional diving seagull.

After wolfing his pasty, Pendragon started running up and down the wharf, trying, unsuccessfully, to catch one of the birds.

"We'll *never* get rid of her . . ." Ravi moaned.

"How long is it going to take her to examine the whole house?" Thomasina asked.

"And, most important of all, what is she going to do when she's finished?" Ravi added bleakly.

They both looked at Minerva, who wrinkled her freckled nose. *That's one problem we're not going to solve easily,* she told herself, skimming the water's surface with her feet. She had thought about it over and over (her hair was a tangled mess, something that always happened whenever she thought hard), but she had not come up with a plan. Luckily for her, she did not have to answer the question just yet.

"Have you come to see the Terror of the Seas?" two silvery voices asked behind them.

Startled, the three children spun around. Araminta and Gwendolyn Bartholomew stood there smiling at them, their faces shaded by two pink, silk parasols.

"Last night old Tom saw it off Shipwreck Bay, you know," Araminta whispered, stooping to talk to them.

"He said that it was huge and sent up sprays of water as high as a mountain," Gwendolyn whispered.

Pendragon started barking at the ocean, as if to dare the monstrous creature.

Ravi yanked on the leash and pulled the dog back. "Don't worry," he spoke softly to the animal. "I'll protect you."

"One thing is for sure," Araminta whispered, "this part of Cornwall never runs out of monsters!"

The sisters were the town historians, and in the summertime, the Bon Ton, their women's clothing shop, turned into a tourist office. They knew almost everything about the small village and its surroundings — and about the people who lived there. Other than fishing, there was very little to do in Pembrose. Therefore, gossip was the townspeople's favorite pastime.

Minerva's face brightened. "What about Lizard Manor?" she asked. "Any mysteries there?" It had occurred to her that the two might know something about the door the Order of the Owls were searching for. In the meantime, without realizing it, she had taken out the small key and started fiddling with it.

The sisters opened their eyes wide.

"Mysteries?" Araminta exclaimed.

"That house is bursting with mysteries!" Gwendolyn chimed in.

"Did you know that it was built with pieces salvaged from sunken ships?" Araminta asked. "That's why it has such an odd shape."

"The wooden rafters, however, rotted from the salt water," Gwendolyn explained. "And the house has always been on the brink of collapse . . ."

"It is not wise to build houses on the bodies of those who died at sea," Araminta concluded grimly.

Steady steps echoed along the wharf as a huge shadow was cast upon them. "My dear ladies, you wouldn't be scaring these poor children with one of your awful stories, now would you?" Doctor Gerald asked in a stern voice.

The sisters startled and blushed. They had been caught red-handed. Telling frightening stories was indeed their specialty.

The Pembrose doctor had a striking presence, and he commanded a sense of awe whenever his black eyebrows plunged into a frown, just like they were doing now. He was the only man in the village who dressed somewhat elegantly and would never leave his house without a necktie. That was one of the reasons why his elderly patients loved him, in addition to the fact that he offered them tea and cookies and always took their ailments very seriously.

The doctor turned to the children. "Do you by any chance know who that strange woman wearing wool socks is?" he asked. "She's not one of my patients, and she doesn't look like a tourist. I bumped into her while she was heading up to Lizard Manor . . ."

"Oh no!" Minerva cried. "We'll be in trouble if she doesn't find anyone there!" She slid the small key back under her collar and stood up, glancing warily at her friends.

Ravi and Thomasina shot to their feet as if their bottoms had been pinched by one of the little crabs that covered the rocks of the jetty.

"Please excuse us, we have to go now!" Minerva said politely. Then she dashed to her bicycle. "Hurry up!" she urged her friends. "I know a shortcut that will get us there before her."

A little dumbfounded, the two women and the doctor stood there staring as the three children mounted their bicycles and took off like rockets.

Upset, Pendragon started barking furiously: they had forgotten about him.

Ravi suddenly stopped, made a U-turn, and darted back to get him. "I'm so sorry!" he said as he secured the dog in the bicycle basket. Then he zipped toward Lizard Manor. The big house stood there waiting for them, perched atop Admiral Rock like a fat spider at the center of its web.

CHaPTer 5

NEVER GO ON
AN ADVENTURE
ALONE!

The following day Thomasina was late meeting her friends. When Ravi saw her walking up the driveway, he was amazed: she was a heavenly vision! The silky, blond curls were held in place by butterfly-shaped hairpins, and she was wearing a delicate dress tied at her waist with a soft ribbon.

"We are hosting a ball at my house tonight," the girl explained. "Mom and Dad really want me to go. But I've already put on my dress, so I can spend more time with you. Do you like it?" She whirled around, and the skirt of the sky-blue dress opened like a magnificent flower.

Pendragon immediately tried to bite the hem.

Ravi was quick to hold the dog back by the collar. "C-cool," he stammered. He looked down at his T-shirt and washed-out jeans. He would never be at her level.

Fortunately, at least Minerva didn't care about her clothes. She was wearing one of her many funny-looking outfits that had belonged to her ancestors. She found the clothing in the chests and wardrobes scattered around the house.

"Where's Mrs. Broomstick?" Thomasina asked glancing around. "Isn't she here yet?"

"Sure she is," Minerva replied. "She's examining kitchen number three."

Lizard Manor had three kitchens. Number one was always flooded and number two was always engulfed in the smoke coming from the wood stove. Therefore, they used only kitchen number three.

"We sneaked out while she was inspecting the refrigerator," Ravi said.

"It'll take her a while, because I've just bought groceries," Minerva said, winking. "We can take a look around for the mysterious door in the meantime."

The three kids raised their eyes to the house that loomed over them. It would take them a long time to search all of it!

Ravi swallowed. He felt even more uneasy after hearing the Bartholomews' story. What still unsettled him most, however, was the manor's name.

"Are you really sure that there are no lizards here?" he asked Minerva for the millionth time.

He just could not stand those little reptiles, especially the fact that they could lose their tails. He had seen it happen once, and it had been a disgusting sight.

"I've already told you," Minerva replied. "Not a single one."

"But . . . what about the one in the puzzle?" Thomasina asked. "Where is that one?"

"That's right. How can we find a door without a lizard?" Ravi exclaimed, worried once again.

In that exact moment, the sunlight reflected off the armpiece from the armor that still lay on the fountain next to the front door. The light caught Minerva's attention.

The girl walked up to take a look at the stone lizard sculpted on the edge of the pool. It was perfect in every detail, so perfect that it looked as if some kind of magic spell had turned it into stone while it was lazily basking in the sun.

"Well, this is actually the only one —" she began but stopped mid-sentence. Something extraordinary was happening.

The shadow cast by a tall, ancient pine tree had reached one of the ground floor windows — one that overlooked the fountain. Half of an owl etched in the glass had turned dark, just like the tail of the stone lizard.

Minerva's nose tingled. *"When the owl is cut in half and the lizard loses its tail, you have found the City of the Ravagers . . ."* she recited aloud. "Oh! I've got it!" she cried, scaring the socks off her friends. Without giving any explanation, she put her hands on the lizard's tail and pushed with every ounce of strength that she could muster up.

At first, nothing happened. Then, screeching loudly, the fountain started to turn, and then it opened, revealing a flight of stairs.

The three friends were frozen with amazement.

Minerva was the first one to shake off the awe. "Hooray!" she exclaimed, raising her arms to the sky in victory. "We've solved the puzzle!"

They could not celebrate for long, though.

"CHILDREEEEN! WHERE ARE YOU?" It was

Mrs. Broomstick. The creaking of her crocodile-skin boots echoed through the entrance hall.

"What are we going to do now?" Thomasina asked. "She's coming!"

Minerva ran a hand through her tangled hair then made a decision. "Come on! Follow me!" she ordered. She stepped into the dark hole that had opened beneath the fountain.

Ravi and Thomasina followed her, with Pendragon close behind them. As soon as they had reached the bottom, though, something unexpected happened: the fountain closed behind them.

When Amelia Broomstick, first-class social worker, craned her neck out the main door, the three kids had vanished.

"*Humph,* that's odd," she grumbled. "I thought I heard their voices."

Ravi put his hand on Pendragon's mouth. *"Shush,"* he said. "She'll hear us."

"We can't let her find us. Not now that we're about to find the door," Minerva whispered.

The three children stood still and silent. When the woman's footsteps had died out, they all breathed a sigh of relief.

"Phew! That was close." Minerva sighed.

"We managed to disappear right under her nose!" Thomasina cheered.

"Where are we though?" Ravi glanced about. "It's too dark to see anything."

Thomasina started rummaging through her bag; she was never separated from it. "We're going to need this," she said, taking out a flashlight. She shone a light on the stairs they had come down from.

Ravi walked to the top and tried to push the wall that had closed up behind them. "Not a chance. It won't budge." He gave up.

"And I can't see any way to open it either," Thomasina observed.

"So we're stuck down here," a worried Ravi said.

Minerva grinned. She didn't look worried at all. "Maybe, but we've solved the puzzle," she reminded him. "So . . ."

"The door must be here!" Thomasina said excitedly. She started sliding the light beam along the wall. "Hey! There's a lamp over there," she said.

An old oil lamp hung on a rusty nail. Two flints for lighting it were set in a small hollow space in the wall next to the lamp.

Minerva rubbed the flints together, until they produced a spark. She lit the lamp, and a moment later they were surrounded by the glow of warm light. "You can put the flashlight away," she told Thomasina.

They could see clearly now: they were in a round space the same size as the fountain.

"Look! It's there!" Ravi cried pointing at something behind the girls.

The two girls turned around and saw a two-shutter wooden door. Its edges were decorated with lizards carved into the wood. The small reptiles looked almost real: tiny hissing tongues, scrawny clawed feet, and bodies that looked like pocket-sized dragons. They were covered in a layer of dark green paint that was now flaking off.

They drew closer to take a better look at it.

"Finally," Thomasina muttered solemnly. "The door to the City of the Ravagers . . ."

"The door to the treasure!" Minerva cheered.

"Okay, but . . . where's the lock?" Ravi asked. "I can't see it."

"Well, it has to be there," Minerva insisted.

They searched every inch of the door but couldn't find anything.

"Rats! I've never heard of a key for a lockless door!" Thomasina groaned. Unable to give in despite the evidence, she kept feeling for the lock on the ragged wood.

Minerva, on the other hand, stopped to think. She took the small golden key in her hand, as if it had the power to inspire her. Her friend was right: if there was a key, then there definitely had to be a lock as well. But where?

"Easy Pendragon! Be a good doggy!" Ravi yelled, trying to hold the dog back. Pendragon wanted to get in on the action.

The animal ignored Ravi. He let out a short growl and flung himself at the door. Then he bit the largest and most real-looking lizard and started shaking it back and forth until it came off revealing . . .

"Wow! The lock!" Thomasina exclaimed.

"Attaboy, Pendragon!" Ravi exulted, hugging the dog and scratching his ears. "You are definitely Agatha's dog!"

An excited Minerva slid the golden key into the lock. It fit perfectly. She looked at her friends, who gestured at her to go on. The girl turned the key three times and then it clicked.

They all held their breath. Slowly, Minerva started pushing the door forward and . . .

"Wait!" Ravi stopped her. "Are we sure there aren't a thousand lizards on the other side? Maybe they were all locked up back there."

"Well, there's only one way to find out," Thomasina pointed out. "Let's go in!"

Ravi sighed, then nodded at Minerva.

"Guys, this is an historic moment for the Order

of the Owls," she said solemnly. And then, her heart throbbing like a jungle drum, she opened the door.

When they found themselves in a little room that contained nothing out of the ordinary, they were very disappointed. It didn't even look like there were other doors.

"You've got to be kidding," an angry Thomasina blurted.

The only thing in the room was a tiny barred window that you could reach only by standing on your toes and stretching. When they looked through it, they saw Mrs. Broomstick's crocodile-skin boots. She was searching for them.

SQUEEEAK! SQUEEEAK! SQUEEEAK!

What could they do now? Ask the evil social worker to help them get out?

"Rats! I can't believe we came all the way down here for nothing!" Thomasina grunted and stomped her patent leather shoe on the floor.

Minerva pricked up her ears. "Did you hear that?" She immediately bent down to examine the spot where Thomasina's foot had left a print in the dust. She started brushing the floor clean with her hands and then blew the rest of the dust away. "There it is! I thought it sounded hollow!" she exclaimed.

Flabbergasted, Ravi and Thomasina stood staring at the floor. Minerva had uncovered the edges of a trapdoor and a small brass ring.

"You're a genius!" Thomasina cheered, hugging her. Then, not caring that she might soil her beautiful dance dress, she squatted and grabbed the brass ring that served as a handle. She looked at her friends with a bright grin. "Are you ready for a new adventure?"

Minerva looked at Ravi. He swallowed, picked up Pendragon, and nodded. "Okay, I'm ready."

Minerva flashed him a smile and then turned to her friend. "Open the trapdoor, Thomasina!"

The girl pulled on the ring. The wooden door came up with an agonizing creaking sound — it had probably been a very long time since someone had last opened it.

Thomasina took the lamp and craned her neck into the black hole that had opened at her feet.

"Wh-what do you see?" a worried Ravi asked.

Thomasina leaned over some more, and then let herself slide into the hole and disappeared.

"Oh no!" Ravi yelled, terrified. He and Minerva rushed over to see what had happened.

"No worries," the girl reassured them. "I'm okay."

Indeed she was: not a curl out of place and not a wrinkle on her pretty blue dress.

The girl held up the lamp to light up the space around her.

She was standing in a coverless rectangular wooden crate. Stuck in the middle of the crate was a metal pole with a ring on the end. A piece of rope was attached to the ring and then ran through a wooden disk. The disk was attached to a bar stuck into the rockwall just above the crate. The other end of the rope came out of the disk and fell back into the black pit underneath the crate.

"It's some kind of hoist," Minerva exclaimed.

"That's right," Thomasina said. "There's a pulley to move it up and down," she explained, pointing at the disk fixed to the metal bar. She reached out and touched the rope hanging out of the crate. "This one's tight. There must be a weight tied to it at the bottom," she decided. "The crate won't go down unless it's heavier than whatever's pulling the rope."

Minerva grinned. "Very well. Let's make it heavier then!" she exclaimed and jumped into the crate, joining her friend.

The hoist swung violently but did not lower by an inch. The two girls raised their eyes to Ravi in expectation.

"You're the only one missing," Minerva said.

"Come on, Ravi! Don't be such a party pooper!" Thomasina chided him.

The boy hesitated, holding Pendragon tight.

"Everything will be all right," Minerva tried to reassure him.

"Come on, what are you waiting for?" Thomasina urged. She winked. "Next stop: City of the Ravagers!"

"And the treasure!" Minerva added. Ravi buried his face into Pendragon's cuddly fur, then he looked at his friends who were smiling at him encouragingly. He decided that he had no choice: sometimes you just had to take a leap of faith.

And leap he did: he closed his eyes and jumped into the crate. The device was easily triggered by his weight, and they immediately began to go down. Faster and faster, wobbling like jelly.

"*Wahoo! Hold ooon!*" Minerva shouted.

"Treasure, here we come!" Thomasina cried.

"C-can't we slow down just a l-little?" Ravi asked, clinging on to Pendragon. The animal's large, furry ears stood straight up, pulled by the air, and the dog started howling.

"No," Minerva answered. "Now we're heavier than the load that was holding the rope," she explained. "We'll stop only when we reach the bottom."

"B-but how long is it going to take to reach the b-bottom?" the boy asked.

Thomasina gently patted him on his shoulder.

"Don't fret, Ravi," she said. "Everything will be fine because we have respected the first rule of adventures."

"Wh-what rule is that?" Ravi asked. The hoist was shaking so badly that he almost bit his tongue.

"Never go on an adventure alone!" Thomasina replied. She placed an arm around his shoulder and did the same with Minerva.

And so, huddled all together, they were ready to face whatever might be waiting for them down below.

CHAPTER 6

OUT OF THE FRYING PAN, INTO THE FIRE

The fall seemed endless. *If we go on like this, we'll get to the center of the Earth!* Ravi thought.

His friends, on the other hand, didn't seem worried at all. The more they shook, the more piercing were their shrills of joy, as if they had been enjoying a rollercoaster ride instead of being on their way to a mysterious — maybe dangerous — destination.

Somewhere along the way the rock tunnel began to narrow until the makeshift elevator suddenly came to a stop so violent that the backlash sent the three kids head over heels. The crate did not crash, though, because the bottom was covered in a thick layer of soft moss.

"Last stop!" Minerva announced and immediately climbed out of the crate to see where they were.

Thomasina was close behind her. "Wow, what a crazy ride!" she said excitedly. She straightened her dress and took a couple of steps forward, holding up the lamp.

Ravi made sure that Pendragon was okay. "We've arrived," he whispered. The dog joyfully licked his face. Then they carefully caught up with the two girls.

Minerva was glancing about in amazement. "I'd say we're at least at the bottom of Admiral Rock," she observed. "Maybe even deeper than that."

"Come on, let's keep moving," Thomasina urged them, anxious to get to the heart of the adventure. "This way!" she said, pointing at a tunnel dug in the rock in front of them. She eagerly took the lead.

For a while they went on in single file, until Thomasina shouted, "STOP!"

"What is it?" Ravi called from the back.

The two girls consulted with each other, then Minerva turned around. "Well," she began, "there's a *little* problem . . ."

"I knew it!" Ravi cried out.

"Nothing to worry about," Thomasina butted in.

"We have already found a solution," Minerva confirmed. "Could you put your hands on my shoulders and follow us without looking down?"

"Why is that?" Ravi asked, suspicious. He made them step aside so he could see what the problem was and was immediately paralyzed. The tunnel suddenly came to an end over a dark chasm, and the only way onward was a narrow stone bridge that hung in the air. The boy stared at the abyss below him. "Forget about it!" he yelled. "You know I'm afraid of heights!"

Thomasina's blue eyes glared at him. "Well, at this point you have two options: you can either go back and find a way to activate the hoist on your own — without a lamp — while Minerva and I go on.

With Pendragon, obviously," she said firmly. "Or," she went on in a more gentle tone, "you can hold your arms around my waist like this," she said, putting Ravi's helpless arms around the ribbon that adorned her beautiful blue dress, "and come with us."

Ravi blushed and felt so dizzy just for being so close to his crush, that he followed her without so much as a complaint.

Minerva, together with Pendragon, followed her friends, whistling merrily.

The bridge was very narrow. Ravi closed his eyes like Minerva had suggested and let Thomasina guide him. Luckily, he was so focused on not messing up the neat ribbon that he didn't notice the many rocks that were falling off the bridge and plummeting into the abyss as they walked on.

Minerva did notice, but she decided not to worry about it. For the time being, at least. "One problem at a time. Isn't that right, Pendragon?" she whispered to the dog.

A problem came up immediately, though.

A bigger rock broke off the bridge, and smaller stones rubbled off and spread over the walkway, making it slippery. Thomasina slid and lost her balance for a moment. She promptly regained it, but to do so she threw out her arms and dropped her bag, which plunged into the darkness and disappeared.

"What happened?" Ravi asked, his eyes still closed.

"Nothing serious," the girl answered. "I dropped my bag." She looked into the void below her and sighed. Unfortunately, they had just lost a number of things that would have been useful for underground survival. *At least we're safe,* she thought as she walked on.

They went on without any other accident until . . .

"Uh-oh," Thomasina said when they got to the other side of the bridge. "Which way do we go now?"

They were standing in front of six different tunnels.

Ravi opened his eyes and, when he realized they were safe, he immediately stepped away from the girl. He blushed as red as a tomato.

"We could toss a coin," Minerva suggested.

Pendragon, however, decided for them by walking straight into the first tunnel to their right.

Ravi rushed after him. "Wait up!" he yelled.

Minerva looked at Thomasina. "I'd say we have no choice," she observed. "We have to follow them."

Her friend nodded, and they both ran after the boy and the dog.

"Pendragon! Stop!" Ravi cried again.

However, the dog had been dying to stretch its limbs after all the time he had been stuck in the crate and then carried in Minerva's arms. So the children simply ran to keep up with his pace. That is why they didn't see the first trap.

It was Thomasina who stepped on the tight trip wire laid on the stony ground: they heard a hiss and then a huge saber fell from above.

"Look out!' Only Minerva's reflexes prevented Thomasina from being cut in half by the sword. Minerva yanked her back by the collar of her dress.

"Wow, that was close!" Thomasina cried.

"Hey! What happened?" Ravi asked. He had finally managed to catch Pendragon and had come back to see what had kept the others behind.

Minerva pointed at the sharp-edged saber that was dangling from the ceiling.

Ravi's face went white. "B-but . . . it wasn't there a minute ago!" he exclaimed.

"Thomasina set off a trap," the girl explained.

"That's right. Your dog picked the right way all right!" Thomasina grunted, unflustered by what had just happened but more than ready to blame Ravi.

"He's not my dog," the boy protested. "He's Agatha's," he pointed out. "Besides, you're the ones who wanted to come down here." In the spur of the moment, he took a couple of steps back and didn't realize that he had stepped on a little lever.

"Nobody made you come!" Thomasina snapped back.

Minerva raised an arm. "Quiet!" she commanded. "Can you hear that weird noise?"

The two kids fell silent. Far away, something was booming between the stone walls.

"It sounds like thunder," Ravi said finally.

"I doubt there's a storm coming," Thomasina replied.

The noise was getting louder, and it really did sound like a thunderstorm. The rumbling was almost unbearable, and then the earth started shaking.

Minerva opened her eyes wide. For once, she was really worried. "LET'S *GOOOOOOOO!*" she cried.

They started running like crazy, but the booms grew even louder.

Holding Pendragon tight, Minerva glanced over her back: large boulders were rolling toward them. "Faster! Faster!" she urged her friends.

Nevertheless, the boulders kept closing in and the tunnel was too narrow to dodge them. Minerva looked around desperately searching for a way out: nothing, just the stone tunnel . . . until she saw a crack in the ground right in front of them.

"Let's jump in there!" she yelled, pointing at the opening. "Come on!"

They all took a long jump and curled up the best they could. The boulders rolled past over their heads. A little later, when the rumbling had died out in the distance, a red-haired head popped out to check if it was safe above.

"It's clear," Minerva said with a sneeze. The rocks had kicked up a large amount of dust.

The four of them crept out of their hiding place and sat down to catch their breath.

"Goodness! That was really close . . ." Minerva sighed.

"I've never run so much in my entire life," a breathless Ravi panted.

Luckily, Thomasina had managed to save the lamp, so they could look at each other. Their faces were dust masks, but their clothes had definitely had it worse: they were crumpled, stained, and smeared with dirt. Thomasina's stunning dance dress was torn to shreds.

The girl looked down at herself. "Oh, well," she said thoughtfully, "it's just as well. I don't even know if I'll make it in time for the dance anyway."

"We don't even know if we'll ever get out of here!" Ravi said. "We must have set off another trap. There are traps all over the place down here. We've got to go back. I don't feel like getting cut to pieces by flying swords or squashed like a bug by boulders."

Minerva ran a hand through her dusty curls and pondered. "You're right. The Ravagers of the Sea must have set up loads of traps to protect their treasure." She looked at Thomasina. "Maybe we had better go back and find out if there is a way to avoid them."

"Well, this is *definitely* the wrong tunnel," Thomasina observed, glancing at Ravi.

"Do you really think the other tunnels are safe?" Ravi grunted.

In the meantime, Minerva had made up her mind. "Let's go back. And please, watch your step."

"Hallelujah! Finally a sensible decision!" Ravi said.

However, he was very disappointed when Minerva, instead of crossing the bridge and going back to the hoist, stopped where the path split into the six tunnels. Her freckled face frowned in concentration. "So, we know that traps are used to protect the treasure from intruders," she said. "However, when the Ravagers of the Sea came down here they must have followed a safe way, with no dangers whatsoever . . ."

Thomasina's eyes lit up. "You're right!"

"Okay. But I'd guess they were the only ones who knew about it," Ravi said.

Minerva looked around as if she were looking for something. Suddenly, she crouched on all fours and started searching the floor. Thinking it was some kind of game, Pendragon set after her, sniffing around like a police dog.

Just when her friends had begun to suspect that she had gone bananas, the girl stopped and used both her hands to tear off pieces of moss from a jutting rock at the entrance of the the third tunnel.

"That's it!" she exclaimed.

"What have you found?" asked Ravi.

"Give me the lamp!" Minerva said to Thomasina.

The girl and Ravi got closer, and she handed Minerva the lamp. Minerva shone a light on the jutting rock. Something was carved into the stone — an X followed by a vertical line: *XI*

"That's eleven in Roman numerals," Thomasina said. "We learned about them in school."

Minerva smirked slyly. "There were eleven Ravagers," she said. "This must be their symbol."

"They used a chisel," Ravi observed as he felt the rock. "The marks are deep and neat."

"If they bothered," Minerva said, "they did it to mark the safest way. No traps."

Enthused, Thomasina picked up the lamp. "Great! Let's go this way then!"

Minerva followed her right away, and finally so did Ravi — but with a heavy heart. Some of what his friend had just said might have been true. But she might have been wrong as well. The problem was that the only way to find out was to keep going. So he called Pendragon with a whistle and started walking. He bent over to whisper in the dog's ears. "Adventures are not as easy as they look, old buddy."

The tunnel went deeper and deeper into the bowels of the earth and Minerva must have been right, because they followed the *XI* marks scattered here and there along the way and went on without so much as a problem. That is until they were knocked down by a violent gust of wind that ripped the lamp from Thomasina's hand and sent it crashing to the ground.

Darkness closed in on them.

"What now?" Ravi shouted.

Now they were in deep trouble.

CHAPTER 7

A FEARLESS KNIGHT

"What are we gonna do?" Ravi urged. "We're done for."

"And the flashlight's in my bag," Thomasina said sadly.

"We won't be able to see the *XI* mark now," Ravi insisted. "We'll walk straight into another trap . . ."

Minerva didn't lose heart. She looked over the lamp. Once she knew for certain that it was useless, she leaned against the wall and took a couple of careful steps toward where the wind had come from. After a bit, she squinted. "Hey. Something's glowing down there!" she said. She went on at a steadier pace, and as she did, she realized that the light at the end of the tunnel was getting brighter.

Her friends caught up with her, and they soon came upon a huge cavity, swept by powerful winds.

"Wow!" a speechless Ravi said. "Where are we?"

They had reached an incredible underground world. Before them lay a body of water, constantly swept by the winds, just like the ocean in a raging storm. All around them, the walls of the cave were covered in gigantic quartz crystals of the oddest shapes: flowers, stars, and randomly cut figures that glistened, reflecting the colors of the rainbow-like prisms.

Mesmerized, Minerva walked up to a diamond-shaped crystal: it really looked like a precious stone. She ran her finger across it and then looked at her hand. Her finger was covered in a thin layer of glittering dust. "Take a look at this!" she cried out. "This dust is glowing. And then the crystals reflect the light." She smelled her finger and then gave it a lick.

"No!" Ravi tried to stop her, but it was too late.

"*Hmm,*" Minerva said. "It tastes just like Timothy's seaweed stew."

"Well, it could actually *be* seaweed," Thomasina pointed out. "After all, we are practically at the bottom of the ocean . . ."

Ravi picked up some of the dust for himself and studied it. "Glowing seaweed," he muttered fascinated.

"There are also glowing fish in the sea," Minerva reminded him. "It might be the same thing."

"Wow! What a place!" Ravi gasped, glancing about. For the first time since the beginning of that adventure, he felt happy. It was like they were in a magical underground garden. "This is the perfect place to have a snack." He sighed. "If only we had a snack . . ." he said sadly, thinking of Mrs. Flopps's strawberry scones.

"I had three chocolate bars in my bag," Thomasina grumbled regretfully. "You're not supposed to start an adventure on an empty stomach, you know."

"Well, there's no point in thinking about it now," Minerva said. "At least we've solved our light problem," she said merrily. "And the sooner we find the treasure, the sooner we can go back home and have a snack!" She spotted the *XI* mark engraved on a red crystal and walked on.

There were other wonderful things to discover down there, like a giant petrified mushroom forest and other weird plants the likes of which they had never seen. Suddenly, the body of water grew bigger and bigger, until it formed a kind of inland sea, which Thomasina was quick to name Thomasina's Ocean.

"Then that over there is Mount Minerva!" her friend said, pointing at a peak full of crystals that shone like diamonds.

"And that's River Ravi!" Ravi exclaimed, leaning over to look at his reflection in a shiny pink creek.

And so, they went on, making up the geography of the world they had discovered. They felt like explorers in a marvelous new continent. They raced to find the next mark of the Ravagers of the Sea, and then they continued on: Thomasina led the pack, then Minerva, and finally Ravi with Pendragon.

Suddenly the wind stopped, and the air became so humid that Ravi and Minerva's hair became all damp and crimped and frizzy. Even Pendragon now looked more like a sheep than like a dog. Strangely, only Thomasina's hair stayed in place.

But where was the City of the Ravagers?

After a while, Thomasina's Ocean stretched out so much that it was impossible to say where it ended. A bluish mist hung over the surface and made it impossible to see farther than three feet from the shore.

The kids grew uneasy again: the adventure had begun to lose its appeal.

"Did you guys notice that we haven't found the *XI* mark for a while?" Ravi said.

"It might be a good sign," Minerva replied. "Maybe we are getting close to the City."

"Or maybe we're lost," Ravi grunted.

"You have to have a little faith when you're on an adventure," Thomasina said with confidence.

"Sometimes you have to get lost, in order to find the right way."

That said, she stepped into what looked like a puddle of mud, but which, in fact, swallowed her up.

"Thomasina!" Ravi screamed. Nothing, however, was left of his crush. Not one single blond curl.

The boy clenched his jaw. It was peculiar, but whenever Thomasina was in danger, he immediately got rid of the fear that usually paralyzed him. On the contrary, he felt more like one of the knights from King Arthur's Round Table.

"Don't go any closer! It's quicksand!" he yelled at Minerva. He glanced around, looking for something that might have been helpful, but he didn't know what he was looking for. He turned around and looked at Minerva who, for once, looked helpless. So he lay on his stomach and leaned over the puddle. "Hold me by my feet," he told his friend.

She nodded and grasped his ankles firmly.

Ravi took a deep breath and slid into the puddle until only his calves stuck out.

Minerva looked at Pendragon, who was desperately barking next to her. "Don't worry," she said. "He's gonna make it. You'll see."

A moment later, she realized that Ravi was twitching, so she pulled with all her strength. The momentum sent her sprawling, pulling both Ravi and Thomasina with her.

Her friend seemed totally unaffected by the recent accident. She ran her hands through her hair to wipe off the mud and said, "Well, you see, sometimes you really have to get into trouble to realize that you are living a true adventure."

Ravi, who lay breathless next to her, sat up all of a sudden. "If you so much as say one more single word about adventures . . ." he scolded her.

She looked at him with her amazing blue Bambi eyes. "Okay, whatever you say, my hero . . ." She sighed and gave him a loud kiss on the cheek.

Red as a tomato, Ravi shot to his feet. "Come on. We've got to get out of here before we all drown in quicksand!"

Since there were no more marks carved in stones to show them the way, they decided to walk along the shore of the inland sea in order to keep their sense of direction. The world around them had suddenly grown more bleak and threatening: the number of shiny crystals decreased, and the unusual plants that surrounded them were now wild and thorny.

Ravi froze. "I have a feeling someone's following us," he whispered.

Minerva stopped next to him and frowned. "I know. I've been having that feeling for a while," she admitted.

They looked around, but all seemed eerily still and silent.

Suddenly there was a loud *SMACK* followed by a series of gurgling sounds.

"What was that?" Thomasina cried out.

They pressed against each other: was the threat coming from the sea or was it coming from the land?

A moment later, Pendragon started barking furiously at the water. The three friends whirled around at once, just in time to catch a glimpse of a set of circles rippling the surface of the water.

"Wh-what was that?" Ravi stammered.

"Something big . . ." Minerva said sternly.

The circles disappeared, but the mysterious sound came from the mist once again, and then the water filled with bubbles, like a pot on a stove.

Ravi's throat knotted. "That's not the Terror of the Seas down there, is it? Maybe this is his house . . ."

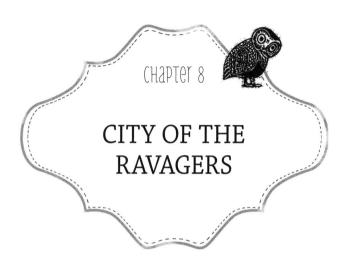

CHAPTER 8

CITY OF THE
RAVAGERS

While our heroes were in the thick of their underground adventure, life in the world above went on as if nothing had happened. Or nearly.

Mrs. Flopps, unaware of the latest developments at Lizard Manor, was gloating because she had managed to sell all her delicious strawberry jams at Truro's farmers' market. She could finally have the holes in the roof fixed!

At Crowley Hall, Thomasina's enormous house, the orchestra was tuning up on the perfectly mowed lawn lined with roses, while trays of delicious finger foods were carefully placed on pressed, starched linen tablecloths.

On Pembrose wharf, a lonely fisherman was scanning the ocean with worry. *Once night falls,* he wondered, w*ill the Terror of the Seas be coming back?*

Things were not much better at Lizard Manor: first-class social worker Amelia Broomstick was looking for the three fugitives under the rhododendron bushes in the garden. Fourteen snowy owls roosting on the roof were spying on her every move. They knew what had happened, but they couldn't tell anybody about it.

* * *

Meanwhile, in the underground world, the members of the Order of the Owls had calmed down a little. They had stood still, closely watching the water for a very long time, but nothing else had happened.

"Let's keep going!" Minerva made up her mind eventually. "It's getting late."

Warily, they kept walking along the shore of the inland sea until they came to a small wharf. And there, tied to a cleat, was a rowboat. It was in perfect condition, and it seemed like it was just there waiting for them.

A gust of wind that smelled like flowers tousled Minerva's hair. She felt as if the breeze was pushing her toward the boat. Without giving it a second thought, she jumped into it.

Ravi looked at her horrified. "You're not seriously thinking of going out into the water?" he exclaimed.

Minerva had already picked up the oars. "Well, this boat is here for a reason, isn't it?"

In the meantime, the boy had leaned down to examine the boat. "Hey, there's something written here . . . a name. Oh, man! The boat's name is *Althea*!"

Minerva opened her eyes wide. Althea, the only woman among the Ravagers of the Sea. She was a charmer who had first mesmerized evil Black Bart and then cursed him to an existence of unending sorrow that would haunt him even in the afterlife!

"It's decided then; we'll continue in this boat," she stated, putting the oars into place.

"Wh-why?" Ravi asked.

"Because it's a sign," Minerva replied. "And my instincts tell me that we have to go over there." She pointed to the mist that hung over the sea.

"But . . . what about the Terror of the Seas?" Ravi reminded her.

"Come on, my hero!" Thomasina urged him, pushing him onto the boat. "If the Terror messes with us, we'll show him what we're capable of!" She untied the lines, and after picking up Pendragon, she jumped in and joined the others, causing the little boat to rock dangerously.

Ravi held on to Minerva to avoid falling into the water. "I'd like to remind you that I can't swim," he said in a voice that was nothing more than a weak whisper.

Minerva handed him the oars. "That's great. You

can row then. That way you won't spend all your time worrying about falling overboard."

They traded places, and Thomasina sat next to Minerva, with Pendragon at her side. "Full steam ahead!" she encouraged Ravi.

The boy decided that there was no point in telling those two that he had never operated a pair of oars in his entire life. He let them slide into the water, hoping not to drop them, and the boat leapt forward like a crazy frog.

"That's perfect," Minerva encouraged him. "Keep it up!"

Ravi repeated the action with great effort. This time the oars hit the water surface with their flat side, whipping up sprays of water so high that they all wound up soaked to the bones.

"Oops! I'm sorry . . ." the boy mumbled, trying to reposition the oars.

Pendragon shook off, but he was so dirty that he splashed the three kids with a mixture of mud and water.

"Perfect," Thomasina said with a sigh. "Just what I needed."

As they continued, the water sprayed, and the boat jumped and jerked. Ravi never took his eyes off the water, for fear of being attacked by the Terror of the Seas. Finally they reached a point where they were completely surrounded by the mist.

"Which way do I go now?" the boy asked. "Any suggestions from your sixth sense?" he sneered at Minerva. But at that precise moment, the boat hit a wooden pole and Ravi fell back, the oars still in his hands.

"I'd say we've arrived," Minerva answered, pleased with herself.

A gentle gust of wind that smelled of wild flowers and the moor began to blow above the water surface. It scattered the mist enough to reveal . . . the City of the Ravagers!

"Wow, I can't believe it!" Thomasina exclaimed. "We found it!" Overcome with joy, she flung herself at Ravi — who was too busy holding the oars to realize what she was doing — and hugged him. "You're the perfect captain!"

Ravi turned red. Wow, two compliments in one single day! Could he finally be close to conquering her heart?

Unfortunately, that was not the right time to get sentimental. They had reached their destination. Or so it seemed.

They were right in the middle of a group of stilt houses. The houses were encrusted with seashells with mother-of-pearl reflections, while the wood stilts were covered in long strands of seaweed.

As quickly as it had come, the strange breeze died down and the mist started thickening again.

Minerva looked around. A big lizard was carved into every door . . . every door but one. "Let's go there," she said, pointing to the lizard-less door.

The boy swallowed. "But . . . how do you know no one's still living there?" he whispered. "A descendant of the Ravagers of the Sea for instance."

"That's a good point," Minerva admitted. She dug

her slingshot from her pocket. Luckily, she had a good amount of acorns. They were now completely surrounded by the mist, but she could still make out the targets. She took aim, pulled the band and hit all the doors, one by one.

The shots echoed like eleven bell tolls, then silence fell.

They stood still and waited for a reaction, but none came and nothing happened. No one showed up on the wharf.

"Not a single soul in sight," Thomasina declared. "Let's go!"

They tied up the boat and and carefully got off. Minerva studied the door. "Hey, there was a lizard here too," she whispered. "It's been rubbed out . . . but you can still make out the outline."

"You're right," Thomasina said. "Very strange. Do you think the treasure is still here?"

They all stared at the door, uncertain of how to go on. Then Pendragon pushed the door open with his muzzle and walked inside.

They followed him and found themselves in a room that smelled like salt. Everything was blue and turquoise: the walls, the hammock that hung from the ceiling, and the large rug that looked as if it were made of seawater. Curtains made from delicate, tiny seashells hung from the windows. Where could the treasure be?

A little writing desk caught Minerva's attention. A curved blade knife was stuck into the wooden table. Its handle had nine beautiful diamond inlays that spelled the letter M. The girl moved closer and saw that someone had carved the word *GOODBYE* on the desk. The blade was stuck exactly in the middle of the letter *O*. A scroll lay next to it.

Puzzled, the three kids stood staring at the writing desk. Ravi was a bit scared of the knife, while Thomasina pointed at the scroll. "Maybe it contains instructions on how to find the treasure," she whispered.

That wasn't the case, though: it was a letter. It was dotted with small smears, as if someone had been crying while reading it. Or maybe they were just time stains, because it sure looked pretty old.

Minerva's eyes jumped to the bottom of the page. "It's signed Althea!" she cried.

Next to the signature, there was a blue wax seal with an owl stamped in its center and the words *Domina Noctuae* written around it.

Minerva picked up the scroll and started reading: *"January 15, 1732, last day of freedom . . ."*

The moment her voice echoed through the blue house, a breeze very much like the one that had scattered the mist, rustled the shells that hung from the windows.

Minerva continued, *"My dear Merrival —"*

"Merrival!" Thomasina interrupted her. "Your ancestor . . . the man in the portrait behind which we found the golden key!"

Minerva nodded and started again: *"My dear Merrival, while you were on your way to Scotland, Black Bart reported me to the Crown Authorities. Therefore, by the time you read these words of mine, they will have already taken me to the Tower of London to carry out my death sentence."* The girl stopped and raised her eyes to look at her friends. They were staring at her, wide-eyed. They were listening to the story of the legendary, enchanting witch.

Minerva lowered her eyes and concentrated on the scroll. *"It is ironic, think you not?"* she resumed. *"I have the power to control the ocean and unleash storms so violent that seafarers aboard their ships shall scream in terror. I have the power to blow the gales that scourge the moor, and I am the wayfarers' nightmare. I can throw huge waves against our coasts and hunt the fish away from the fisherman's nets. The owls obey me and serve as my messengers. I can foretell both luck and misfortune. All these arts I have learned on my own and with great sacrifice. However, I was helpless against Black Bart and his wicked nature!*

I now understand what a terrible mistake it was to join the Ravagers of the Sea: they have forever slain whatever little good was in me. From then on, my destiny was decided and my punishment inevitable.

The only justification I can find is that I was a poor and ambitious orphan, and I thought that a girl like me would have never made it in this world without help from men. In the end, I have paid for my mistake dearly.

However, I have taken my vengeance upon old Bart! I surely did! It was me who won at last! Not only did I cast a curse upon him that will haunt him until the end of time, but I have also managed to steal the only thing he ever cared about right from under his nose: his treasure!

I am sorry, but none of you Ravagers of the Sea will ever find it.

I forgive you for not doing anything to defend me. You were scared of Black Bart, that boastful braggart, and could not find the courage to tell him that you were in love with me. We should have left like we had planned, just you and I, headed for wherever the wind would have taken us, far away from here. A new world. Forever free.

But you were weak. You lost me. That shall be your punishment.

As far as our newborn baby girl is concerned, she is in a secluded place now. I have found some good people who will raise her. I cannot reveal their identity, though: it is the only way to keep her safe from Black Bart and the other Ravagers.

I left her a hint to locate the treasure and also a very powerful amulet that will protect her from HIM. My one and only hope is that the treasure will grant her a better destiny than the one her mother had. At least, she will not have to ask anyone anything. She shall be free and independent.

I cannot say more.

Goodbye my only love.

Forever yours,

Althea

Minerva closed her eyes and pressed the scroll against her chest. She sniffed the air: the brackish smell had been replaced with a pleasant scent of heather and wild flowers. The fragrance, however, suddenly vanished, and the curtain went still once again.

Althea had gone forever.

Minerva opened her eyes and placed the scroll next to the knife. "Goodbye," she whispered, tracing the word carved on the wooden table with her finger.

Her friends had listened to her silently, their mouths hanging open, but they were clearly about to burst.

"Wow!" Ravi said. "So Merrival used his knife to carve that word when he found Althea's letter. And he must have cried too," he added, studying the specks on the scroll. "That means he really loved her, even if he didn't leave with her . . ." Lately, Ravi had been particularly interested in the pangs of love.

"Your ancestor Merrival and Althea had a baby," Thomasina chimed in, staring at Minerva. "That baby is one your ancestors . . . and so is Althea! She must be your great-great-great-grandmother." Thomasina tried to calculate in vain. "It's unbelievable! You descend from a witch and one of the Ravagers of the Sea!" she cheered enthusiastically.

"And next to Althea's signature is a seal with the image of an owl," Minerva muttered thoughtfully, running her finger along the edges of the wax seal. "And this inscription: *Domina Noctuae*. We must find out what it means."

"The treasure's not here, though." Ravi brought them back to reality. "Althea stole it before she was locked up in the Tower of London."

"That's right, to get back at Black Bart," Thomasina said. "I wonder if her daughter ever found it," she said. "She had just been born when she lost her mother."

Minerva shook her head. There were still so many mysteries to solve.

Ravi looked a bit disappointed. "We came all the way down here for nothing."

"Well, we've just had an amazing adventure!" Thomasina replied.

"And it is not over yet!" Minerva added. She studied the writing desk. There were other things in addition to the knife and the scroll. Books on flowers, plants, and marine animals. A pair of leather gloves, a snow-white linen handkerchief, and an amethyst pendant. The dark purple stone had a heather flower embossed on it.

The girl's eyes lingered on a little box. Something was written on the lid. *"Take one leaf and stress you will vanquish, take three and memories will vanish,"* she read. She opened it. Inside were small leaves that looked like tea leaves.

Thomasina bent down to smell them. "Mmm, they smell like licorice."

"They smell more like mint to me," Ravi said.

Minerva dipped her nose in the little box. "I'd say they smell like strawberry!" Then, a playful light flickered in her eyes. She closed the box and put it in her pocket. "This will come in handy for something I have in mind," she muttered, but said no more.

Ravi squinted at her. Minerva liked to play the mysterious type. *Now that she's found out that she descends from a witch and a pirate, I wonder how many crazy ideas she'll come up with!* he thought, imagining the worst.

The girl studied the room, as if she were trying to take a mental photograph. Then she said, "Let's go back home. We've discovered all there was to find down here."

They went back to the wharf and got back into the boat. Thomasina untied the lines, while Ravi took his place at the oars. They were all so buried in their thoughts that they became aware of the danger only when it was too late.

Pendragon sensed something was off and started barking. At that point, however, there was nothing left to do. There was a terrible *BANG,* and the boat almost capsized.

"The Terror of the Seas!" Ravi yelled. "It's attacking us!"

CHAPTER 9

TWO EXTRA LARGE FRIENDS!

The water around the small boat gurgled as if they were sitting on top of an erupting volcano. Afraid to drop them, Ravi squeezed the oars. He closed his eyes: he didn't want to see a giant octopus or a crab-shaped sea creature take aim at them.

The boat bobbed and shook so violently that it looked like a nutshell at the mercy of a storm.

The boy squeezed his eyes even tighter. *That's it. We're done for!* he thought. A moment later, though, the water calmed again. "What's going on?" he asked, keeping his eyes closed. In answer, he was hit in the

face by a spray of water. Then he heard someone
giggle. "Wh-what . . ." he cried, opening his eyes wide.
His words, however, died on his lips.

"Surprise!" Minerva said.

"Look what it is!" Thomasina exclaimed.

A long, shiny snout popped up next to their
boat. The creature's mouth was opened as if it were
smiling over a successful prank.

"Whoa! It's a-a wh-whale!" Ravi cried out, amazed.

"That's right! It's a calf, a baby," said Thomasina.

Another spray hit Ravi in the face. It seemed like
the young whale was trying to introduce itself. The
water came from the blowhole at the top of its head.

"Hey!" the boy exclaimed. "Enough already!"

The calf wasn't through, though. It was enjoying some sort of game. It sprung out of the water and dove down again. It reappeared soon after with another spectacular leap that drenched the sailors, including Pendragon, who barked his discontent.

Ravi wiped the soaked hair off his face. "What's a whale doing down here?" he asked, amazed.

Just as if it had understood the question, the baby whale went under once more, not completely though: its tail emerged from the surface and pointed at the opposite way they were going.

"I think it wants us to follow it," Minerva said.

Ravi was skeptical. "You talk whalese now? Why should we follow it?"

"Maybe it knows another way out," Thomasina guessed.

"That's exactly what I was thinking," Minerva replied. "We're at sea level now, more or less. There might be a way out to the ocean. After all, the whale must have come from somewhere."

Ravi turned to look at the whale, which had stopped a little ways ahead of them, as if waiting. When the whale looked at the kids, it really seemed like it was smiling, as if their presence made it happy. "Okay," Ravi said, somewhat softened by what he was seeing. He dipped the oars in the water. "Let's do as you say."

Among jerks and abrupt stops (he would need lots of practice to finally learn how to row properly), the boy followed the tail that emerged from the water. In that part of the inland sea, the immense cavity they were in was quite dark, and it was very hard to say where they were going.

The small whale went on without any problem. At times, however, it couldn't help itself and would either leap out of the water or shake its tail. The problem was that, though a baby, it still measured more than ten feet in length and its playfulness caused massive waves. Ravi had a hard time steering the boat so as to keep out of the way of their excited new friend.

After a while, their guide swam into a tunnel. It was very narrow, but the small boat fit smoothly, even though the passengers had to duck to avoid bumping their heads against the ceiling. Less than half a yard farther down, they caught a glimpse of the exit and of the sun's shiny reflection on the water.

"Hooray! We did it!" Minerva cheered, hugging Thomasina, who was sitting next to her.

Ravi said nothing. He was doing his best to maintain control of the boat in that tight space, but he felt relieved when he saw the open sea. He even thought he heard the seagulls cawing, and that familiar sound made him feel rejuvenated. He rowed decidedly until the tunnel started getting even narrower.

At that point, they had to pull in the oars and make their way out by pulling on the protruding stones. They were lucky for once, since the tide was going their way.

Minerva glanced around. "I bet the cliff collapsed here and opened a passage. It probably wasn't here when the Ravagers of the Sea were around."

When they finally got out of the tunnel and into the open water, they were almost blinded by sunlight. A gentle salty breeze tickled their skin, and the rhythmic sound of the waves soothed them. They were in the middle of a small nook between Admiral Rock and the cape where Pembrose stood.

Ravi finally felt the tension leave his body and smiled at the sight of the familiar surroundings. The wind-lashed cliffs, the ocean, the sky, and the clouds had never looked more beautiful to him. "Wow! What a journey!" He sighed.

"Bravo, Ravi!" Minerva complimented him. "You've been a great captain!"

"You could even sail in the open sea now," Thomasina said.

Ravi stiffened: he was done with boats as far as he was concerned.

"Look up there! It's Lizard Manor!" Minerva exclaimed, pointing at the cliff behind their backs. "Once we reach the shore, we can walk up to it."

Ravi let out another sigh of relief and dipped

the oars in the water. The boat, however, stopped abruptly. "Aw, what's happening now?" he grunted, annoyed.

Minerva shaded her eyes with her hand and scanned the water surface. "We're stuck in fishing nets," she said. "There are lots of them around here."

"Hey! Our friend has stopped too," Thomasina said. They turned to look at the baby whale.

"It can't reach the open water," Minerva said. "It's trapped in the nets. You know, I heard sailors down at the harbor say that the nets pose a real danger for small whales."

Before they could do anything, another surprise greeted them.

"Whoa! Wh-what is that?" Ravi shouted, jumping to his feet and rocking the boat as he did so.

Out in the distance, a spray of water so high and powerful that it looked like a geyser shot up from the surface. Then a huge gray whale jumped out of the water, and for a moment, it seemed to be pulling the whole ocean up with it.

The children, who had never seen an adult whale before, felt very, very small at the sight of that amazing creature.

"Oh, b-boy!" an overwhelmed Ravi stuttered.

Minerva grinned. "That must be the mommy whale."

The humongous animal resurfaced in front of the nets and started pushing with its snout.

"It's trying to free its baby," Ravi observed. He stopped in mid-sentence and his jaw dropped. "That means . . ."

"That's right," Minerva continued for him. "We have found the Terror of the Seas."

"You mean it was the mother whale then who ripped the nets trying to free its baby?" Thomasina asked.

Minerva looked at the calf. "The baby must have found a way to get up to here, but then it couldn't get back to the open water."

"And all this time its mommy never left it . . ." Thomasina added.

"The fishermen saw the mother," Minerva continued, "and mistook it for the Terror of the Seas."

"Come to think of it," her friend interrupted her. "I read somewhere that whales migrate north during summer." She shifted her eyes from the mother to its baby. "How are they going to do that?"

Minerva ran her fingers through her hair, which was practically one big knot at this point. "We'll help them," she decided.

* * *

It was not easy, but with a lot of patience and with Ravi manning the oars, Minerva and Thomasina managed to move the nets aside enough to let the baby whale through.

Then, they stood and watched mother and baby swim out into the open water. The pair had almost reached the end of the bay, when the small whale stopped, turned toward them, and flashed that funny smile that Ravi knew so well by now.

"Goodbye!" he cried, waving.

"Have a nice trip!" Minerva yelled.

"Say hi to Greenland for me," Thomasina shouted. "And please, watch out for fishing nets!"

Even Pendragon barked three times.

The little whale caught up with its mother, and they both breached out of the water, almost touching the sky. When they fell back down with a huge splash, they disappeared from their sight forever.

Feeling a bit lonely, Ravi put Pendragon on his knees and rowed to a narrow shore just below Admiral Rock. They beached the boat far enough inland so that the tide would not drag it away, then they started walking up the hill toward Minerva's house.

They looked like four castaways. Their clothes were tattered and soaked, but, all things considered, they felt happy.

"The Order of the Owl has done a great job today!" Thomasina said happily as they lumbered along the stony path. "We have solved two mysteries. Number one — we found the City of the Ravagers, and number two — we revealed the real identity of the Terror of the Seas."

"We also saved the baby whale!" Ravi chimed in.

"And we also found out that Althea is my great-great-great-grandmother," Minerva added, glancing over her back, toward the boat that was named after her mysterious ancestor.

"We still don't know where the treasure is, though," Thomasina remarked. A complete success would have made her much happier.

Trying to distract Thomasina from her disappointment, Minerva made a suggestion. "Hey! The last one who gets to the house will fix snacks for everybody!"

At the mere thought of snacks, Ravi's stomach started growling like a bear (after all, they hadn't had lunch), and he took off like a rocket. He got there first, but when he reached the back of the house through a hole in a garden hedge, he stopped in his tracks.

"What's wrong?" asked Thomasina, who was right behind him with Pendragon. But she needed no answer. She immediately understood why Ravi had stopped.

SQUEEEAK! SQUEEEAK! went the boots of first-class social worker Amelia Broomstick.

"Oh no!" Thomasina whispered. "I almost completely forgot about her."

"I didn't," Minerva muttered. "Come with me — we can't let her see us like this."

They snuck into the house through the back door. Minerva opened a storage bench and fished out some clothes. "Put these on," she said quietly.

The clothes were out of fashion, but they were clean and in fine condition.

They quickly slipped into their new outfits and looked at each other to judge the outcome: Ravi looked like an eighteenth-century knight, with his knee breeches and buckle shoes, while Minerva's cute dress was completed by a ribbon-adorned hat.

Thomasina did a quick twirl: she looked lovely in her Empire-waisted dress. "Perfect! I'm ready for my parents' ball," she whispered.

SQUEEEAK! SQUEEEAK! The boots echoed through the corridor that led to the entrance hall. All of a sudden, Mrs. Broomstick appeared before them. She looked somewhat sweaty in her wool dress, but the bun in her hair was perfect.

"*Humph,* there you are at last!" she exclaimed. "Where have you been? I've been looking for you all day!"

Minerva gave her a big smile. "Oh, we're really terribly sorry, but we were helping Mrs. Flopps . . . she's uh . . . she's repairing the rainwater well today." Minerva tried to ignore her tickling feet while she made up her story. "To apologize for disappearing like that, we'll make you some tea," she suggested. "Would you mind waiting for us in living room number four please?" she said, gently pushing her toward the door.

There were no foxes in living room four, and the furniture was even intact, even though the sofa was sagging a bit.

Minerva and her friends vanished to kitchen number three before the woman had a chance to say anything.

"What do you have in mind?" Ravi asked Minerva, as she put the kettle on the stove and got the strawberry jam from the refrigerator.

"Wait and see," Minerva said mysteriously. She warmed the last of the scones that Mrs. Flopps had made.

"Can I have just one?" Ravi asked after a while, yearningly eyeing the trayful of warm scones. "I'm starving."

"Later," Minerva replied. She rummaged in her pocket and dug out the little box that she had taken from Althea's writing desk and dropped three leaves into the teapot. "*Mmm,*" she said, savoring the scent that the leaves gave off. "All right! Tea's ready!" she announced, picking up the heavy tray loaded with treats. She served the tea in the living room, on a wobbly coffee table.

The social worker slumped down onto the couch and put the bag, where she kept her crocodile-leather notepad and Minerva's file, on the floor. "*Humph . . .*" she said, sniffing at the puffy cloud of steam rising from the cup of tea. "It smells like peppermint," she remarked and had a sip.

Minerva watched her closely, and so did Ravi and

Thomasina, who were still wondering what their friend was up to.

"*Humph,* delicious," Mrs. Broomstick finally said. "Why . . . who are you?" she asked a moment later, looking a bit confused.

Minerva glanced mischieviously at the other two and secretly showed them the label on the cover of the little box.

Ravi silently read the instructions: *Take one leaf and stress you will vanquish, take three and memories will vanish.*

"You're a genius!" Thomasina whispered.

"Some more tea?" Minerva asked the social worker, refilling her cup.

"*Humph,* thank you," she said, drinking it up. "Why am I here?" she asked, looking around.

"You came to look at the house. You were thinking of buying it," Minerva reminded her, grinning politely.

"That's correct. You said it's not really your kind of house, though," Ravi continued, playing along.

"Because it's too big," Thomasina added.

Minerva gently patted the tweed-covered shoulder pad. "We were enjoying a cup of tea all together before you headed back home . . ."

"To Good Manners Alley, in London," Ravi reminded her, snatching three scones.

Once they had finished their tea, they quickly showed her to the door, under the yellow eyes of fourteen snowy owls that spied on them suspiciously.

"You'll get your memory back soon, don't worry," Minerva comforted her.

"It must have been the heat," Thomasina said.

"The village is at the bottom of the hill," Ravi said. "Look for the Fishbone Inn."

"Have a nice trip!" Minerva shouted, while the woman lumbered down the path. Then she showed her friends something that she was hiding behind her back.

"Your file!" Ravi cried. "How did you manage to take it from her?"

"I just slipped it out of her bag while she was drinking her tea — piece of cake," Minerva replied, winking at them. She held it to her chest and said softly, "Thanks, Althea . . ."

"What are you going to do with it?" Thomasina asked.

"Well, it was hidden behind a file cabinet for so many years," Minerva said with a spark in her eyes. "I guess no one was meant to find it." She tore it up into a thousand little pieces and threw them up in the air like confetti. "There you go. No more trouble from London Central Office!"

With Pendragon following behind, they chased the tiny pieces of paper as the wind scattered them across the garden and over to the edge of the cliff. They stood there, watching the pieces of paper flutter over the open sea and then head north, just like the whales had done.

"Hooray!" Minerva and Thomasina cheered in unison.

Ravi squinted at his curly, red-haired friend and felt a wave of relief flow through his body: she would not be sent away!

CHAPTER 10

THE DRAGON
DARE

"*Ow!* I'm gonna explode!" Ravi moaned, rolling over on his back and slapping his stomach. "I ate like a pig," he said and let out an extremely loud burp. "Oops! Pardon me!"

His friends burst into laughter.

"You've also got the manners of a pig," Thomasina remarked. She was perfect, as usual, in the sea-green dress they had found at Lizard Manor along with a matching pair of satin shoes.

On the other hand, Minerva's mouth was all

smeared with jam. She also had some on the tip of her freckled nose.

They were all lying on the grass after finishing a *huge* snack. Their picnic blanket had been covered with all kinds of delicious food: jam and whipped cream scones, saffron cake, and rye bread slices topped with fresh butter and sugar.

"Boy, I felt like I hadn't eaten in days." Ravi sighed, gazing at the blue sky dotted here and there by strings of clouds that looked like cotton candy.

"Give me a break!" Thomasina grunted. "We were gone for just half a day."

"It felt like forever to me," Ravi replied, suddenly feeling exhausted.

"That's because so many things have happened," Minerva explained, licking a speck of jam off her chin.

Thomasina's blue eyes gleamed. "Right. Our successes today . . ." she began. She liked to keep track of all their adventures in her special book. "We found the door and the City of the Ravagers," she started listing. "We saved a baby whale, and we got rid of Mrs. Broomstick," she concluded. "Failures," she resumed less enthusiastically. "I lost my bag, unfortunately, and . . . we haven't found the treasure."

"We'll find it," said Minerva confidently. She rolled over on her stomach and studied the small golden key. It shone brightly in the sun like a promise.

"You forgot the most important mystery," Ravi added. His friends turned to look at him.

Ravi smiled, happy to have the last word for once. "I'm talking about the mystery of Minerva's origins," he explained.

"That's right, and we must find out what happened to Althea and Merrival's daughter," Thomasina admitted. "If we follow her track, it may lead us to the treasure and —"

"To my parents!" Minerva finished, her eyes shining.

"Hush, someone's coming!" Ravi warned them. He had noticed that Pendragon was growing restless.

Indeed, the dog had pulled its ears back and started barking. Then he dashed toward the gate.

Alarmed, the three friends immediately stood up.

"*Ugh!* What now?" Ravi grunted, resigned to face another disaster. When he saw Agatha get out of her Jeep, however, he heaved a sigh of relief.

"Hi, children!" she cried, waving at them. She looked gorgeous with the blue sky in the background and her long black hair lifted by the wind.

They all ran to her, but Pendragon arrived first. Agatha picked him up, spinning him around. "Oh! I missed you!" she cried. "But I'm sure you took good care of him." She laughed, turning to the children.

They exchanged an embarrassed look: to be perfectly honest, they had put the dog in all sorts of danger. Fortunately, though, all had ended well, so they didn't have to say anything about it.

As if she had sensed that something was not quite right, a light went on in Agatha's eyes. It lasted just a moment, though, and her smile immediately came back. "This is for you," she said, handing a letter to Minerva. "I found it in the mailbox near the front gate. Your name's on it."

"Really?" Minerva was very surprised. They never got any mail at Lizard Manor, except for the bills that they never had the money for.

Agatha hugged Pendragon. "I see you guys just had a snack," she said, pointing at the blanket and what was left of their feast. "If you come see me at my house in the moor, I'll bake you an amazing cake," she said. "Secret witch recipe."

Ravi turned pale: that was not a cake he wanted to try. He didn't want to be rude, though, so he replied, "Oh, I'm sure it'll be delicious!" He shot a sideways look to Minerva, who was already giggling, and added, "Besides, I'd like to come see Pendragon." And that was true. He was going to miss his friend a lot. "Goodbye," he whispered to the dog, stroking his head between his long, fluffy ears. "Don't forget me."

Pendragon looked at him with his big, dark eyes and licked his hand.

"Thanks for everything," Agatha said. "I'll be expecting you soon then." She turned to leave but then stopped, as if she had remembered something.

"Be careful," she said at last. Then, for a brief moment, a shadow ran across her face. She seemed to be about to say something more, but then, as if she had changed her mind, she walked toward her truck.

Minerva was too concerned with her envelope to notice Agatha's behavior. She couldn't wait to see what was inside. Her heart throbbed painfully for a moment: could it be a letter from her parents?

"Well, what are you waiting for?" Thomasina encouraged her.

"Don't you want to know who sent it to you?" Ravi asked. He was dying to know.

Minerva tore the envelope open and took out a sheet, which she read in one single breath. When she raised her eyes to look at her friends, she had a concerned look on her face.

"What does it say?" Ravi asked.

"It sounds like . . . a dare," Minerva replied, perplexed. "That's what I think, at least. Listen. *He who's found the key and thinks himself wise shall not rejoice for long, for another'll get the prize!*"

The girl scratched her nose, musing. "Signed: *The Dragon.*"

"What?" Ravi said, surprised. "Let me see . . ."

Thomasina craned her neck to read the letter.

"I don't get it," Ravi said. "Who's this Dragon? Why would he want to dare us?"

"And how does he know that we've got the key?" Thomasina added.

"Well, I'm sure the Bartholomew sisters saw it," Ravi said. "That day at the wharf. And they like to talk so much . . . maybe they told the whole village."

"That means the Dragon could be anybody in Pembrose . . ." Minerva muttered.

Thomasina's eyes shone. "Wow! Another mystery! But we like a challenge, don't we?"

"We love it!" Minerva confirmed.

Ravi shook his head. There they went again. When all he wanted was just another bite of that yummy saffron cake. "Aren't you supposed to go to your parents' ball?" he asked Thomasina to divert her attention from that new mystery.

"Rats! I'd forgotten about it!" the girl exclaimed, slapping herself on the forehead. She looked at her friend and studied him from head to toe.

Ravi blushed. "What?" he grunted. "What's wrong with me now?"

"Nothing at all," Thomasina replied. "You know what? You look pretty good in that outfit. You look like a prince. Will you be my date to the ball?"

Ravi blushed red. He knew that boys usually asked girls to things like that. Adventure-loving girls like Thomasina, however, always took the initiative.

"Great," she said matter-of-factly, not bothering to wait for an answer. She slid her gentle little hand under Ravi's arm. "Let us go, my fair prince!" she said.

Ravi made a choked sound but then obediently followed her.

Thomasina turned to Minerva. "You should come as well! Come on!" she encouraged her. "We're going to play pranks on the more boring guests."

Minerva shook her head. "Mrs. Flopps is coming on the six o'clock bus," she replied. "I promised I would be here waiting for her." She waved them goodbye. "I'll see you tomorrow!" she cried.

On the horizon, the sky had taken on a purple shade. Minerva stopped and closed her eyes. She let the gentle breeze caress her face. It felt as soft as a whisper and smelled of wild flowers and heather. A light gust tousled her red curls and swung around her like an embrace, and then it moved toward the sea.

Minerva opened her eyes and smiled: for a moment she had felt like Althea had been there with her.

ELISA PURICELLI GUERRA

As a child, I had red hair. With my red hair, I wanted to be Pippi Longstocking for two reasons. The first was that I wanted to have the strength to lift a horse! The second was that every night my mother read Astrid Lindgren's books to me. As I fell asleep each night,

I hoped to wake up at Villa Villacolle. Instead, I found myself in Milan. What a disappointment!

After all of Lindgren's books were read and reread, my mother refused to read them again. So I began to tell my own stories, each more intricate than the one before and chock-full of interesting characters. Pity then, the next morning, when I would always forget everything. At that point I had no choice; I started to read myself.

Today my hair is less red, but reading is still my favorite pastime. Pity it is not a profession because it would be perfect for me!

GABO LEÓN BERNSTEIN

I was born in Buenos Aires, Argentina, and have had to overcome many obstacles to become an illustrator.

"You cannot draw there," my mom said to me, pointing to the wall that was smeared.

"You cannot draw there," the teacher said to me, pointing to the school book that was messed.

"Draw where you want to . . . but you were supposed to hand over the pictures last week," my publishers say to me, pointing to the calendar.

Currently I illustrate children's books, and I'm interested in video games and animation projects. The more I try to learn to play the violin, the more I am convinced that illustrating is my life and my passion. My cat and the neighbors rejoice in it.

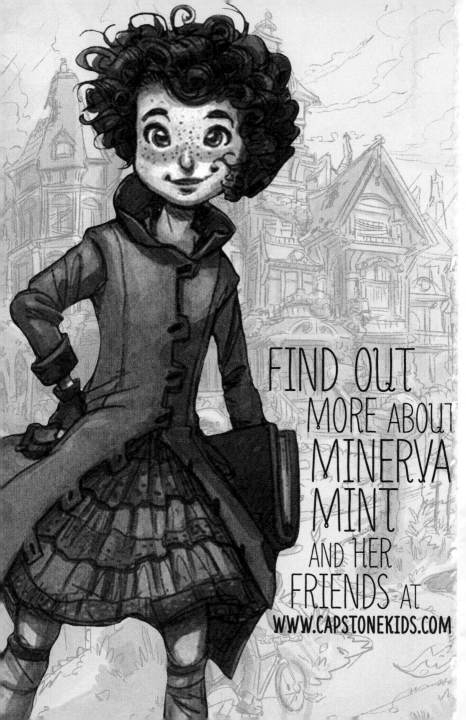

FIND OUT MORE ABOUT MINERVA MINT AND HER FRIENDS AT WWW.CAPSTONEKIDS.COM